D0714914

M.P. Rob⟨⟩ ⟨wr⟩itten and illustrated many picture books including
Seven Ways to C⟨⟩ ⟨⟩on, *The Sandcastle*, *The Egg* and *The Dragon Snatcher*.
He lives in Bradford o⟨⟩ ⟨n⟩ear Bath, with his partner Sophy Williams (also an illustrator)
and their two ⟨⟩ ⟨⟩*d Chain* was shortlisted for the English 4-11 awards.

To Angus, for his help
with the ending.

Food Chain copyright © Frances Lincoln Limited 2009
Text and illustrations copyright © Mark Robertson 2009

First published in Great Britain in 2009 and in the USA in 2010 by
Frances Lincoln Children's Books, 4 Torriano Mews, Torriano Avenue,
London NW5 2RZ

www.franceslincoln.com

First paperback published in Great Britain in 2012

A catalogue record for this book is available from the British Library.

ISBN: 978-1-84780-165-4

Illustrated with pen and watercolour

Set in Couchlover

Printed in Shenzhen, Guangdong, China by C&C Offset Printing in June 2011

9 8 7 6 5 4 3 2 1

Find out more about M. P. Robertson's books at www.mprobertson.com

FOOD CHAIN

M.P. Robertson

F

FRANCES LINCOLN
CHILDREN'S BOOKS

Little fish,

naughty little boy!

Naughty
little boy,

evil plan!

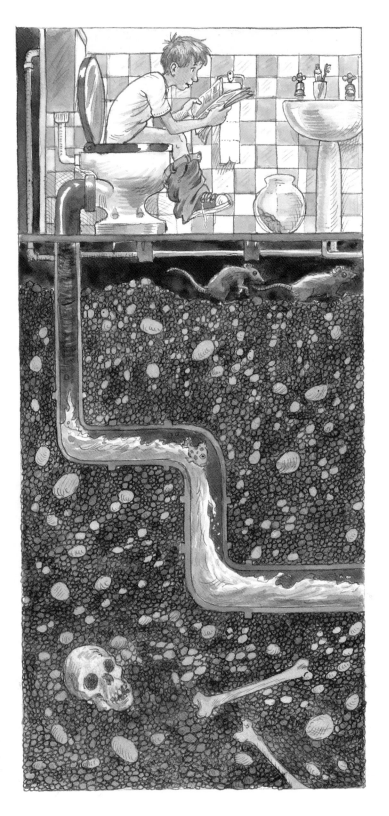
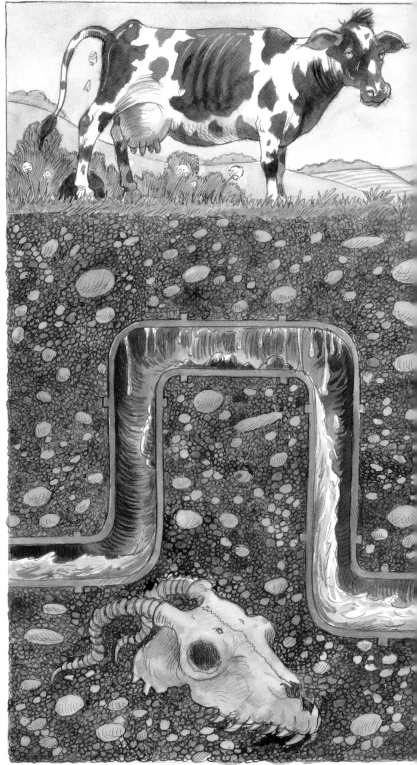

Little fish,

long smelly pipe.

Little fish,
BiG OCEAN.

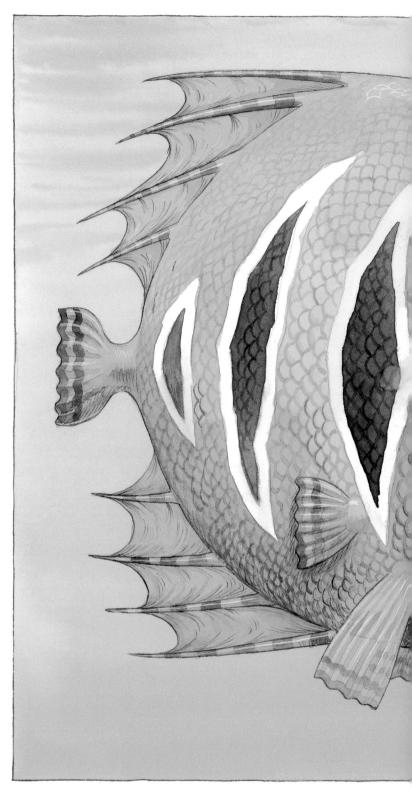

Little fish,

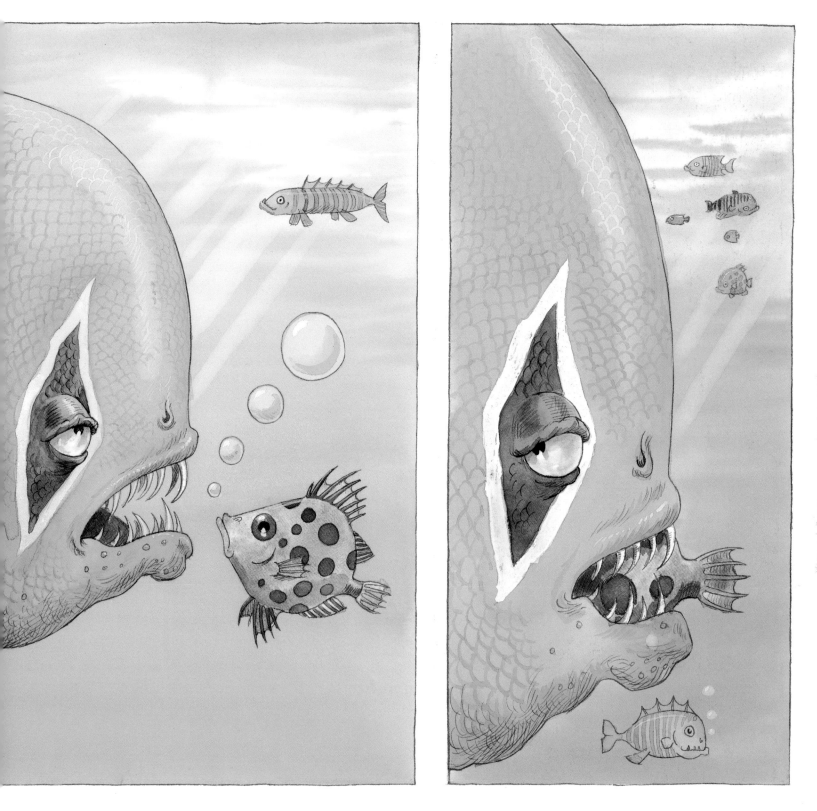

BIG FISH!

BIG FISH, BIGGER FISH.

BIGGER FISH,
GREAT
BIG FISH.

GREAT
BiG
FiSH,
little worm.

Great big fish,
BIG PLUMP
FISHERMAN.

FISH & CHIPS,

naughty little boy!

Naughty little boy,

BIG OCEAN.

Naughty little boy,

GREAT BiG HUNGRY WHALE.

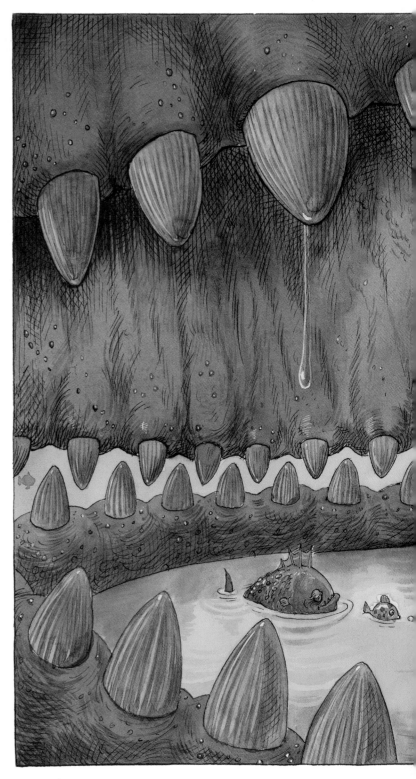

Naughty little boy,

NARROW ESCAPE!

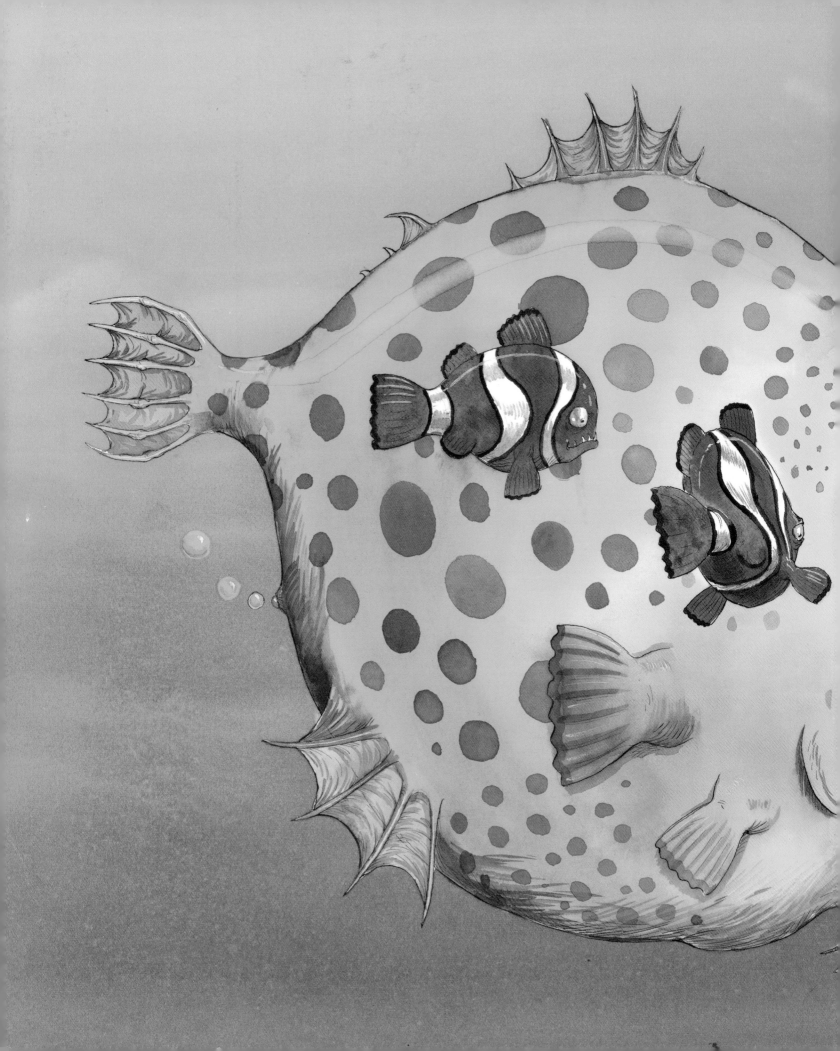

MORE TITLES BY M.P. ROBERTSON FROM
FRANCES LINCOLN CHILDREN'S BOOKS

THE EGG

When George discovers a rather large egg under
his mother's favourite chicken, he soon finds himself
looking after a baby dragon and giving lessons in
How to Distress a Damsel and How to Duff a Knight. . .
A fantastic story of adventure and discovery with
gloriously atmospheric illustrations.

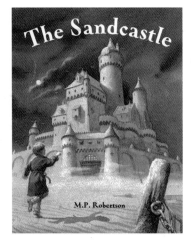

THE SANDCASTLE

Jack loves building sandcastles more than anything
in the world. One day he finds a shell with magical
powers, and makes a wish to be king of his own
sandcastle. In no time he finds himself in the middle
of an amazing adventure. But is his new power
greater than the power of the sea?

HIERONYMUS BETTS AND HIS UNUSUAL PETS

Hieronymus Betts has some very unusual pets.
But he knows of something that is slimier, noisier,
greedier, scarier, and stranger than all of them
put together. But what on earth could it be?
Dare you read this book to find out?